COLOUR Yorkshire

Published by Bradwell Books, 11 Orgreave Close, Sheffield S13 9NP.

Email: books@bradwellbooks.co.uk

British Library Cataloguing in Publication Data:
a catalogue record for this book is available from the British Library.

1st Edition

ISBN 9781912060733

Design and typesetting by: Andy Caffrey

Images traced by: Brian Marriott

Image Credits: All images referenced individually.

Print: Hobbs the Printers, Totton Hants.

BRADWELL BOOKS

USE THESE CAMEOS TO TRY YOUR COLOUR PALLETTE

IF YOU WOULD LIKE SOME INSPIRATION FOR COLOURS, VISIT THE COLOURING BOOKS PAGE AT BRADWELLBOOKS.CO.UK

The village of Yockenthwaite lies in the Langstrothdale valley in the Yorkshire Dales National Park.

ANDY & SUSAN CAFFREY

USE THESE CAMEOS TO TRY YOUR COLOUR PALLETTE
IF YOU WOULD LIKE SOME INSPIRATION FOR COLOURS, VISIT THE COLOURING BOOKS PAGE AT BRADWELLBOOKS.CO.UK

Bolton Abbey lies in the heart of the Yorkshire Dales near Skipton.

IAN CAPPER, USED UNDER THE CREATIVE COMMONS LICENCE

USE THESE CAMEOS TO TRY YOUR COLOUR PALLETTE

IF YOU WOULD LIKE SOME INSPIRATION FOR COLOURS, VISIT THE COLOURING BOOKS PAGE AT BRADWELLBOOKS.CO.UK

From its imposing position on the hillside, Bolton Castle looks across the valley in Wensleydale.

UNKNOWN PHOTOGRAPHER, USED UNDER THE CREATIVE COMMONS LICENCE

USE THESE CAMEOS TO TRY YOUR COLOUR PALLETTE
IF YOU WOULD LIKE SOME INSPIRATION FOR COLOURS, VISIT THE COLOURING BOOKS PAGE AT BRADWELLBOOKS.CO.UK

Grosmont Station on the North York Moors Railway.

UNKNOWN PHOTOGRAPHER, USED UNDER THE CREATIVE COMMONS LICENCE

GROSMONT

76079

USE THESE CAMEOS TO TRY YOUR COLOUR PALLETTE
IF YOU WOULD LIKE SOME INSPIRATION FOR COLOURS, VISIT THE COLOURING BOOKS PAGE AT BRADWELLBOOKS.CO.UK

The Grand Hotel Scarborough, from the Spa Bridge.

UNKNOWN PHOTOGRAPHER, USED UNDER THE CREATIVE COMMONS LICENCE

USE THESE CAMEOS TO TRY YOUR COLOUR PALLETTE

IF YOU WOULD LIKE SOME INSPIRATION FOR COLOURS, VISIT THE COLOURING BOOKS PAGE AT BRADWELLBOOKS.CO.UK

Staithes Harbour on the east coast of North Yorkshire.

ANDY & SUSAN CAFFREY

USE THESE CAMEOS TO TRY YOUR COLOUR PALLETTE
IF YOU WOULD LIKE SOME INSPIRATION FOR COLOURS, VISIT THE COLOURING BOOKS PAGE AT BRADWELLBOOKS.CO.UK

The exit to Whitby Harbour showing the lighthouses on the east and west piers.

BAZ RICHARDSON

USE THESE CAMEOS TO TRY YOUR COLOUR PALLETTE

IF YOU WOULD LIKE SOME INSPIRATION FOR COLOURS, VISIT THE COLOURING BOOKS PAGE AT BRADWELLBOOKS.CO.UK

A Yorkshiremans favourite pastime.

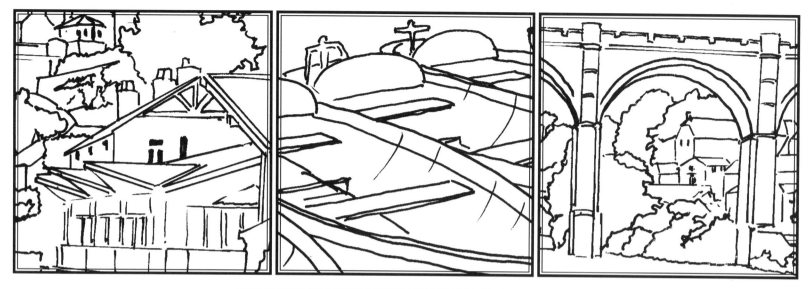

USE THESE CAMEOS TO TRY YOUR COLOUR PALLETTE
IF YOU WOULD LIKE SOME INSPIRATION FOR COLOURS, VISIT THE COLOURING BOOKS PAGE AT BRADWELLBOOKS.CO.UK

Rail Bridge at Knaresborough with boats on the River Nibb.

UNKNOWN PHOTOGRAPHER, USED UNDER THE CREATIVE COMMONS LICENCE

USE THESE CAMEOS TO TRY YOUR COLOUR PALLETTE
IF YOU WOULD LIKE SOME INSPIRATION FOR COLOURS, VISIT THE COLOURING BOOKS PAGE AT BRADWELLBOOKS.CO.UK

The famous Bettys Café & Tea Rooms in Harrogate.

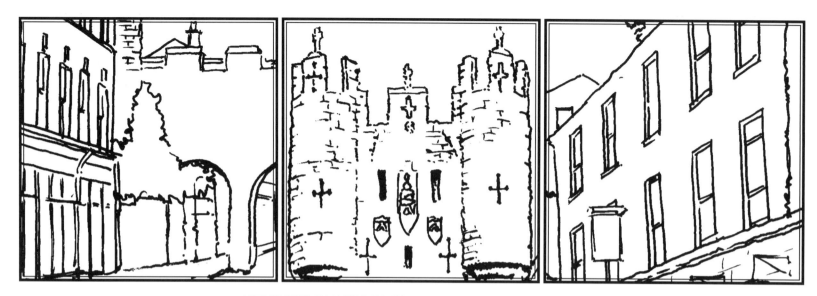

USE THESE CAMEOS TO TRY YOUR COLOUR PALLETTE

IF YOU WOULD LIKE SOME INSPIRATION FOR COLOURS, VISIT THE COLOURING BOOKS PAGE AT BRADWELLBOOKS.CO.UK

Micklegate Bar in the ancient City of York.

UNKNOWN PHOTOGRAPHER, USED UNDER THE CREATIVE COMMONS LICENCE

USE THESE CAMEOS TO TRY YOUR COLOUR PALLETTE

IF YOU WOULD LIKE SOME INSPIRATION FOR COLOURS, VISIT THE COLOURING BOOKS PAGE AT BRADWELLBOOKS.CO.UK

The Racehorse Hotel at Kettlewell.

ANDY & SUSAN CAFFREY

USE THESE CAMEOS TO TRY YOUR COLOUR PALLETTE

IF YOU WOULD LIKE SOME INSPIRATION FOR COLOURS, VISIT THE COLOURING BOOKS PAGE AT BRADWELLBOOKS.CO.UK

Main Street in Dent, which is located in the Yorkshire Dales National Park.

BAZ RICHARDSON

HAWES   14
INGLETON   17
VIA NEWBY-HEAD 7½

USE THESE CAMEOS TO TRY YOUR COLOUR PALLETTE
IF YOU WOULD LIKE SOME INSPIRATION FOR COLOURS, VISIT THE COLOURING BOOKS PAGE AT BRADWELLBOOKS.CO.UK

A visit to Scarborough wouldn't be complete
with a ride along the beach on a donkey!

BAZ RICHARDSON

USE THESE CAMEOS TO TRY YOUR COLOUR PALLETTE
IF YOU WOULD LIKE SOME INSPIRATION FOR COLOURS, VISIT THE COLOURING BOOKS PAGE AT BRADWELLBOOKS.CO.UK

The main road through Hawes in North Yorkshire.

BAZ RICHARDSON

AVAILABLE NOW

BRADWELL'S BOOK OF YORKSHIRE
ISBN13: 9781909914728

BRADWELL'S IMAGES OF THE YORKSHIRE DALES
ISBN13: 9781909914766

BRADWELL'S LONGER WALKS IN THE YORKSHIRE DALES
ISBN13: 9781910551622

BRADWELL'S POCKET WALKING GUIDES YORKSHIRE DALES
ISBN13: 9781910551943

LEGENDS & FOLKLORE YORKSHIRE
ISBN13: 9781912060719

PHOTOGRAPHIC HIGHLIGHTS OF THE YORKSHIRE DALES
ISBN13: 9781902674926

PHOTOGRAPHIC HIGHLIGHTS OF THE YORKSHIRE DALES
ISBN13: 9781902674919

WALKS FOR ALL AGES IN YORKSHIRE DALES
ISBN13: 9781909914179

WALKS FOR ALL AGES SOUTH YORKSHIRE
ISBN13: 9781912060726

WALKS FOR ALL AGES WEST YORKSHIRE
ISBN13: 9781909914780

YORKSHIRE DIALECT
ISBN13: 9781902674650

YORKSHIRE GHOST STORIES
ISBN13: 9781909914049

YORKSHIRE MURDER STORIES
ISBN13: 9781910551196

YORKSHIRE WIT & HUMOUR: PACKED WITH FUN FOR ALL THE FAMILY
ISBN13: 9781902674612

BRADWELL'S IMAGES OF THE NORTH YORK MOORS
ISBN13: 9781912060634

WALKS FOR ALL AGES NORTH YORK MOORS
ISBN13: 9781910551844